We Can Share It!

Written by Sarah Tatler
Illustrated by Bo Sterk

GoodYearBooks

One day Monkey found a long
rope under a tree.
"Ooh, I'm going to play with this
all by myself," he said.

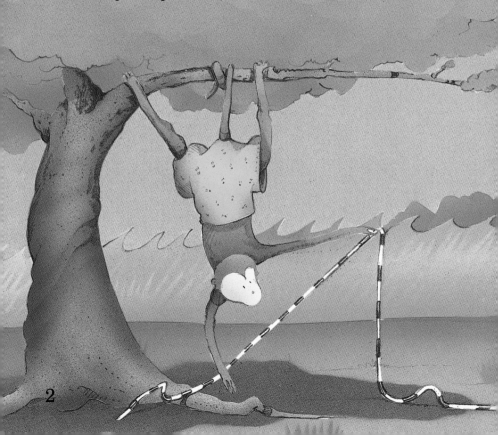

But just before he did . . . .

Swish! Swish! Caw! Caw!
Parrot came flying by.

"Can I have some rope?"
asked Parrot.

"We can share it. I'll cut the rope in two pieces," said Monkey.

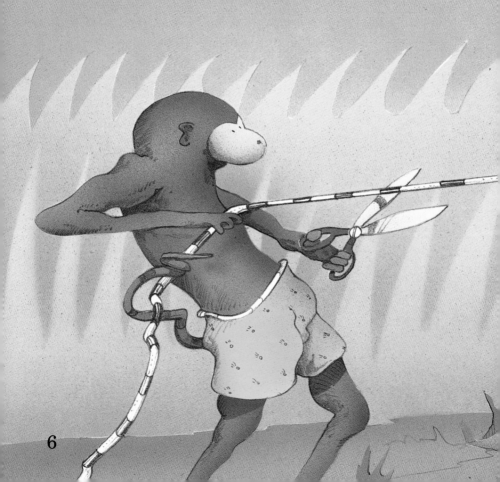

But just before he did . . . .

Boom! Boom! Honk! Honk!
Elephant came thumping by.

"Can I have some rope?"
asked Elephant.

9

"We can share it. I'll cut the rope in three pieces," said Monkey.

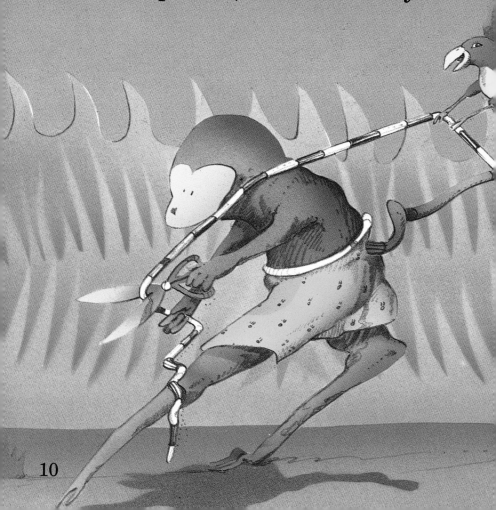

But just before he did . . . .

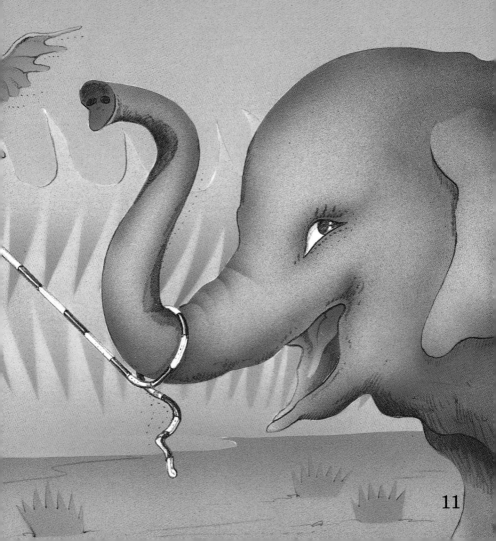

Wiggle! Wiggle! Hiss! Hiss!
Snake came slithering by.

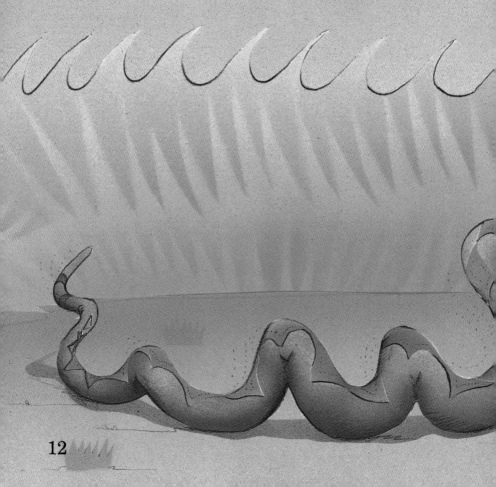

"Can I have some rope?"
asked Snake.

"Oh dear," said Monkey,
  "the rope will be too small if I give
  everyone a piece."

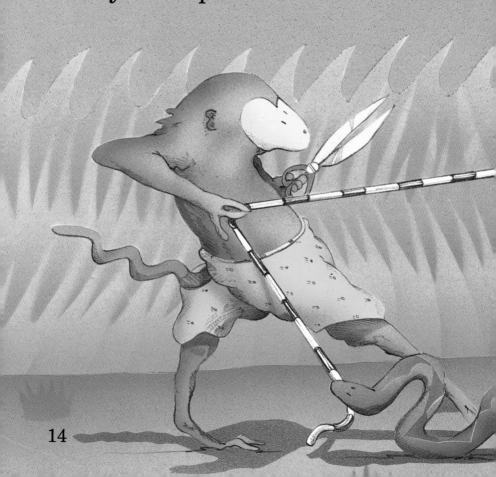

"I know how we can share it," said Parrot.

Get ready!
Get set!
Jump right in!